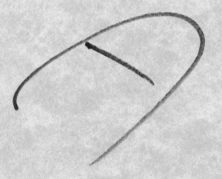

A Snake in the House

BY FAITH McNULTY · ILLUSTRATED BY TED RAND

SCHOLASTIC INC. · *New York*

Library of Congress Cataloging-in-Publication Data

McNulty, Faith.
A snake in the house / by Faith McNulty; illustrated by Ted Rand.
p.   cm.
Summary: An escaped snake finds many clever places to hide
throughout a house, while the boy who brought him home
continues to search for him.
ISBN 0-590-44758-0
[1. Snakes — Fiction.] I. Rand, Ted, ill. II. Title.
PZ7.M24Sn   1994
[E] — dc20   92-27939
CIP
AC

12 11 10 9 8 7 6 5 4 3 2 1   4 5 6 7 8 9/0

Printed in the U.S.A.   36

First Scholastic printing, February 1994

Designed by Claire B. Counihan

The paintings in this book
are watercolors.

To Kellan McNulty
— F.M.

On a sweet morning in May,
a snake stretched out on the shore
of a pond to enjoy the sun.
The warmth felt good.
The snake felt calm.
It did not see or hear the hunter.

The hunter was a boy.
He carried a jar.
He was looking for something to catch.
Anything. Anything alive would
be exciting to catch —
and fun to keep and own.

The boy saw beetles whirling
on the water. But he hoped
for bigger prey.
A frog? A baby turtle?
He walked softly. Hoping. Hoping.

The snake dozed,
and did not hear the hunter.

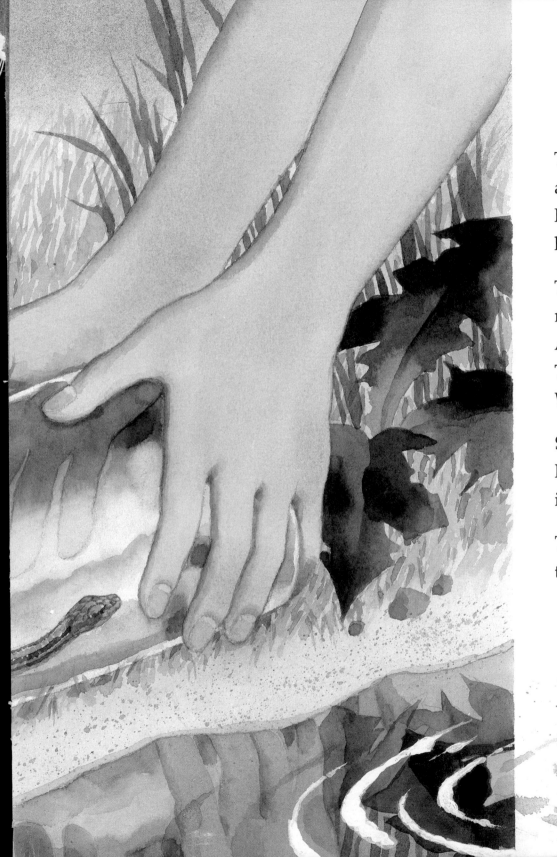

The boy looked down
and saw the snake — almost at his feet.
He stared at it, and
his heart beat fast.

The snake was small,
no bigger around than a pencil.
And no longer than two pencils end to end.
The boy had never touched a snake.
Would it feel cold? Slippery? Would it bite?

Slowly, carefully, he squatted down.
He put the jar on the ground, on its side,
in front of the snake.

The snake awoke. It darted forward
to escape and darted right into the jar.

The boy clapped on the lid and ran home.

Inside the jar, the snake coiled
as small as possible.
The jar shook — knocking him about.
Then the jar was still.
The boy had put it on the kitchen table.

The snake, frozen with fear, coiled at the bottom of the jar.

All around it the glass glittered like water.
The snake's tongue darted out, touching it.
The glass tasted like stone.
The snake looked through and saw a huge face
with round eyes and a hungry mouth.

The boy peered at the snake.
He saw how magically it moved
its slender body.
He saw a snake with pretty yellow stripes along its tan body,
a pale belly, shiny black eyes, and a flickering tongue.

The snake heard loud, terrifying sounds.
The boy was talking to his mother.

"Can we look in the attic for a cage?
Please, Mom," the boy was saying.
Then the snake heard the footsteps of
the boy and his mother going away.

The snake uncoiled. Its nose slid up the smooth,
cold glass, searching for an opening . . . a crevice, a crack;
any way to escape its prison.
The glass was smooth and hard.

At last, when the snake had stretched up
almost as far as it could reach,
its nose touched the metal lid.
The snake pushed harder, and the lid lifted a little.
And lifted more. It fell off the jar.

Frightened, the snake dropped
back to the bottom of the jar
and coiled up. . . .
After a while it lifted itself again,
stretching up and up.
It reached the top of the jar
and slid over the rim . . . and over . . . and down . . .
and dropped onto the table.

The snake heard feet and
voices coming nearer.
It slid off the table
and dropped to the floor.
"Mom!" the boy shouted. "He's gone!
He got out of the jar!"
"Oh, dear!" his mother said.
"Now we have a snake loose in the house.
Please try to find him. Hurry!"

Swiftly the snake glided along
the floor. Looking for a hiding place,
it found one, the space under the sink.
It darted in and slipped under a pile of rags.

The boy looked around on the floor.
He looked under the sink.
He picked up a can of cleanser.
He picked up a box of soap flakes.
He lifted a pile of rags.
No snake.

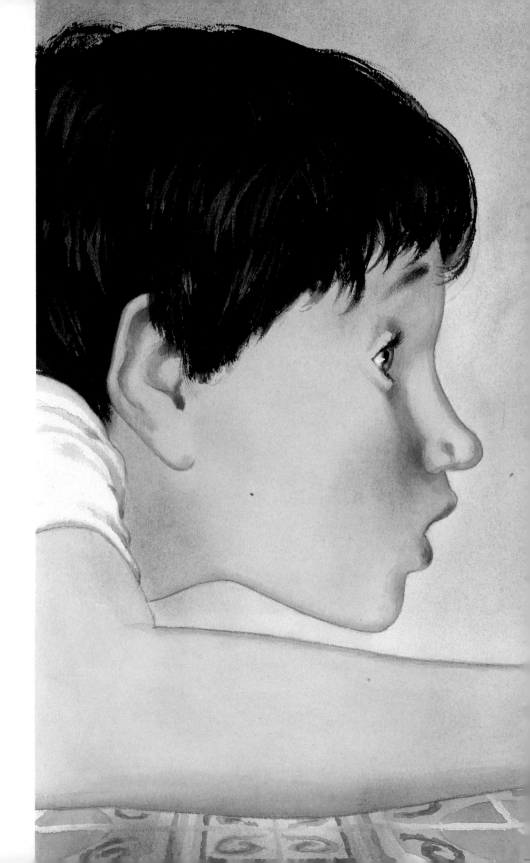

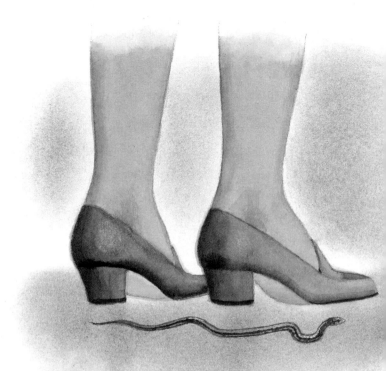

It had left the rag pile and
coiled behind a pipe.
It lay there, quietly — invisible.

"Keep looking," the boy's mother said,
"while I do the dishes."
Water roared and the pipe became warm,
then very hot.
The snake moved out.
It glided past a pair of shoes —
with ankles rising like tree trunks —
to a cupboard where pots were kept.
It coiled up in a frying pan.

It hid there until — suddenly —
the boy's mother lifted the pan.
She screamed . . . and dropped the pan.
The snake slid out and into a colander.

"Get him!" cried his mother.
"Catch that snake!"
The boy peered into the cupboard
and shifted the pots around.

The snake left the colander
and found a small hole in the cupboard
that led to a space under the stove.

"He's disappeared," the boy said.
"I hope you find him," his mother said,
"and when you do, I want you to put him
back where he belongs. My kitchen is
no place for a snake."

The snake stayed under the stove
all night long. At dawn,
it came out and explored, searching
for a way out, a way back to the pond.
It looked for grass and earth and dampness;
small bugs to eat, water to drink,
sunshine to bask in.

Instead, it found floors that smelled of wax,
rugs that were prickly, a box of sand that smelled of cat.
The house was as dry as a desert,
with almost nothing for a snake to eat or drink.

Day after day, the snake searched for a way home.
When footsteps shook the floor
and voices sounded,
the snake coiled in the nearest dark place.

When there was quiet,
it nosed along baseboards, in and out of cupboards,
under chairs and tables.
Now and then it ate a spider.
Spiders are dry and bitter food.
It drank the beads of water on the pipe
under the sink.
The boy kept searching, too.
"Where on earth could that snake be?"
his mother said as she tossed
some boots into a corner,
nearly hitting the snake,
coiled inside an old sneaker.

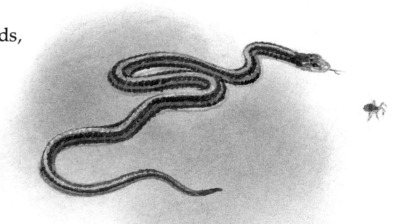

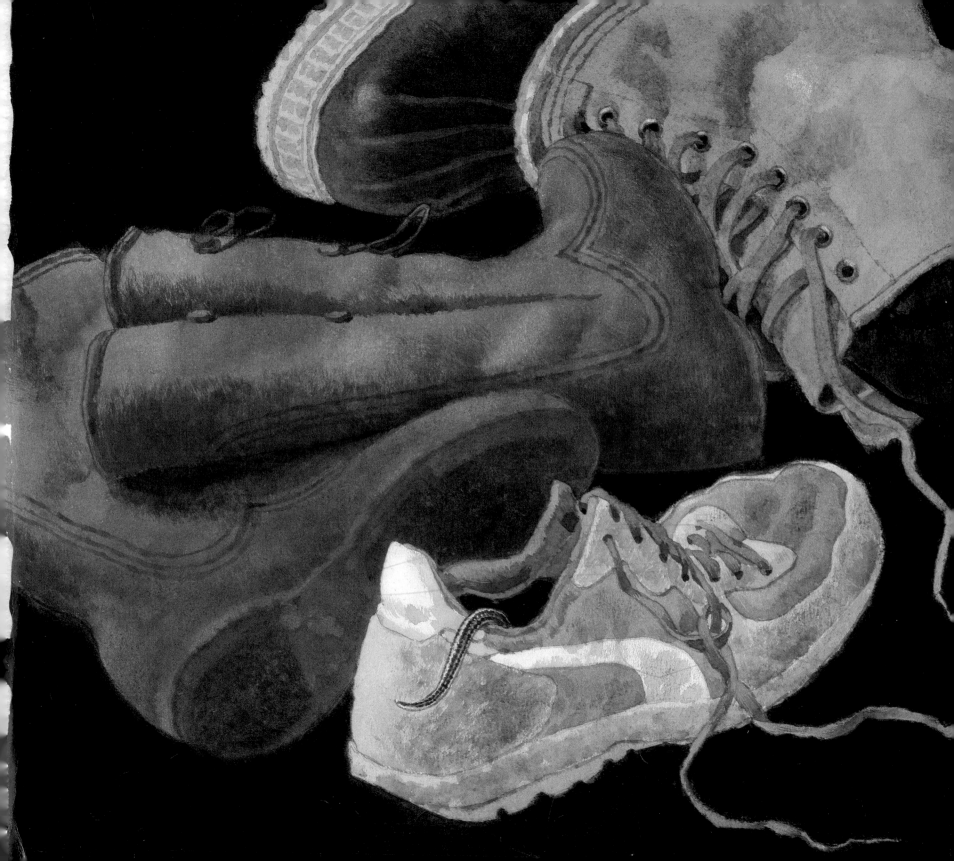

The snake narrowly escaped the cat,
who could smell it, and kept sniffing around
wherever it hid.
"I wonder what Daisy is after," said the boy's mother
as the cat tried to pull the snake
out from under a stuffed chair.
The snake escaped by sliding up into the springs.

The snake was under a bookcase
when the boy's mother
got out the vacuum cleaner.
The noise was terrifying. Even worse
was the end of the hose, poking under
the bookcase like an enormous snake
ravenously searching for food.
The little snake felt its sucking breath
and was barely able to slide into a corner
out of reach.

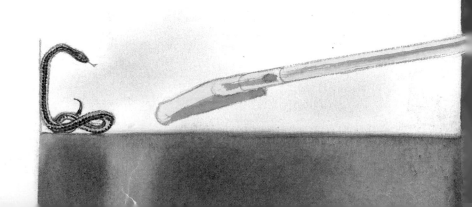

On another day the snake hid in a
sewing basket.
The boy's mother picked up the basket
and put it on her lap.
The snake remained coiled under a sock
while she sewed.
At last she put the basket back on a shelf
and the snake slid out.
Sometimes the boy wondered where
the snake could be.
He searched the pond shore,
looking for another snake,
but caught nothing. Even the frogs got away.

He decided to try fishing.

He dug up some earthworms and put them in a can.

He put the can in a basket and went to
look for a hook and line.

The snake happened to be under a coatrack nearby.

It smelled the damp earth in the can. It glided to the basket
and entered through a hole.

The boy picked up the basket and
walked down to the pond.

At the shore, the boy put the basket
on the grass. Looking into the
dark water, he imagined a huge fish
waiting there.

Inside the basket, the snake smelled the
sweet fresh smell of pond water and moss.
It quickly uncoiled.

The boy saw it and started in surprise.
Now the snake was circling
inside the basket,
searching for the hole.

But the hole had been stopped up
by a crumpled rag.
The boy's hand hovered over the snake,
ready to grab,
but he had never touched a snake
and was afraid.

The snake was climbing the side
of the basket
when the boy's courage returned.
He grabbed the snake and held it tight.
The snake twisted and thrashed,
trying desperately to get free.

The boy held the thrashing body tight.
It didn't feel cold or slimy.
It felt warm and dry and alive.
Very, very alive.
There was so much power in its tiny body;
its will to be free was so strong,
that the boy, in amazement, let go.

The snake dropped from his hand
into the grass.
It disappeared,
hidden by the long stems.
The boy saw the grass ripple
as the snake
glided swiftly away.

For an instant the boy imagined himself
gliding like a snake
through a cool, green forest of grass.

He shared its joy
at being home.